Karen's Toothache

Look for these
and other books about Karen
in the
Baby-sitters Little Sister series:

Little Sister

Karen's Toothache

Ann M. Martin

Illustrations by Susan Tang

A
LITTLE APPLE
PAPERBACK

SCHOLASTIC INC.
New York Toronto London Auckland Sydney

The author would like to thank Dr. Vincent Celenza for his advice and consultation while preparing this manuscript—and for making dental visits as pain-free as possible.

ISBN 0-590-46912-6

12 11 10 9 8 7 6 5 4 3 2 1   3 4 5 6 7 8/9

Printed in the U.S.A.   40

First Scholastic printing, November 1993

*The author gratefully acknowledges
Stephanie Calmenson
for her help
with this book.*

Karen's Toothache

Madame Valerie

"You will grow green antennae on your head."
"The man in the moon will visit you tonight."
"You will grant your sister three big wishes."

"No way! Those fortunes are goofy," said Andrew.

"They are not," I replied.

I was writing fortunes in my Cootie Bug. A Cootie Bug, in case you do not know, is a piece of paper folded a special way, with fortunes written inside. I make excellent Cootie Bugs, even if Andrew does not think so.

Andrew is my little brother. He is four.

I am Karen Brewer. I am seven. I have blonde hair, blue eyes, and some freckles, and I wear glasses.

Andrew and I were in the playroom at Mommy's house. We had already finished eating dinner. And I had finished my homework.

The TV was on. A lady came on the screen and said, "Hello, everyone. I am Madame Valerie, your local fortune-teller. Have you questions about your future? I can answer them all."

I could see that Madame Valerie was a real and true fortune-teller. She was wearing a long skirt, a lacy blouse, lots of beads and bracelets, and gigundo gold hoop earrings.

Madame Valerie waved her hands over a shiny crystal ball. She gazed into it. Then she squinted. (Maybe she needed glasses, like me.)

"Ah, yes. I can see it all now!" she said. "Good news awaits you at sunrise. But look for trouble when the moon is full."

Hmm. Watching Madame Valerie gave me an idea. When the show was over, I turned off the TV and got busy.

I searched the shelves in the playroom. Boy, were they a mess.

"What are you looking for?" asked Andrew.

"You will see," I replied mysteriously. Then I cried, "I found it!"

I held up an old snow globe. It was a souvenir Mommy brought back for me and Andrew from Denver, Colorado. Some little plastic people were inside it. But that did not matter. It would make a fine crystal ball.

Next I found our Magic Eight Ball. It said *yes*, or *no*, or *maybe so*, when you turned it over.

The last thing I found was our Ouija board. That was a very important thing for a fortune-teller to have.

I lined up my fortune-telling equipment. Crystal ball. Eight Ball. Ouija board. Not bad, I thought. (I decided that if anyone asked about the people in my crystal ball, I would tell them they were my fortune-telling advisors.)

I was getting ready to ask my Ouija board a question. But something was bothering me. It was a tooth at the back of my mouth. I set the Ouija board down.

Yesterday my tooth had felt funny when I ate chocolate chip ice cream. Tonight it hurt a little at dinner when I chewed on a carrot. I hoped I did not have a cavity.

I decided not to think about my tooth. I decided to think about my weekend instead. The next day was Friday. Andrew and I were going to Daddy's house. And my toothache was not invited!

What Is a Two-Two?

Mommy's house. Daddy's house. Little house. Big house. Andrew and I have two houses. I will tell you why.

When we were little, Mommy and Daddy got divorced. They loved Andrew and me very much. But they did not love each other enough to live together anymore.

So Daddy stayed in our big house. (That is where he grew up.) And Mommy moved to a little house. Both houses are in Stoneybrook, Connecticut.

Andrew and I live with Mommy most of

the time. But we live with Daddy every other weekend, and on some holidays and vacations.

After the divorce, Mommy got married again. The man she married is Seth Engle. He is my stepfather. He is very nice. When he came to live with us, he brought his two pets. Rocky is a cat. Midgie is a dog. Now they are our pets, too.

Daddy got married again also. He married a woman named Elizabeth Thomas. Now she is my stepmother. When she moved into Daddy's house, she brought four children from her first marriage. They are David Michael, who is seven; Sam and Charlie, who are so old they are in high school; and Kristy, who is thirteen and one of my favorite people ever. They are my stepbrothers and stepsister.

I have one other sister. She is Emily Michelle. Daddy and Elizabeth adopted her from a country called Vietnam. She is two and a half. (I named my pet rat, Emily Junior, after her. Emily Junior lives at the little house.)

Nannie is Elizabeth's mother. That makes her my stepgrandmother. She lives at the big house, too, and helps take care of Emily Michelle.

These are the pets at the big house: Shannon, David Michael's great, big Bernese mountain dog puppy; Boo-Boo, Daddy's meanie cat; Crystal Light the Second, my goldfish; and Goldfishie, Andrew's polar bear. (Just kidding! Goldfishie is really another goldfish.)

I have a special name for my brother and me. I call us Andrew Two-Two and Karen Two-Two. What is a two-two? A two-two is anyone like us who has two houses, two families, and two of lots of other things.

For example, we each have two bicycles — one at each house — and two sets of clothes. That is so we don't have to keep bringing everything back and forth. I have two stuffed cats. Moosie lives at the big house. Goosie lives at the little house. I even have two pieces of Tickly, my special blanket.

Plus, I have two best friends. Nancy Dawes lives next door to Mommy's house. Hannie Papadakis lives across the street and one house over from Daddy's house. We go to the same school, Stoneybrook Academy. We are in the same class. Our teacher is Ms. Colman. And we like to do everything together. We call ourselves the Three Musketeers.

Having two of lots of things is all right. But you do not want to have two toothaches. One of those is plenty.

Karen's Horoscope

It was Sunday morning at the big house. I was sitting at the table with Daddy, David Michael, Nannie, Kristy, and Andrew. We were eating breakfast and reading the newspaper. I felt very grown-up.

I used to think newspapers were boring. Then Hannie, Nancy, and I started one for kids called the *3M Gazette*. Now *that* was interesting. We stopped publishing it, though, because we needed the time for our school work.

But guess what. A friend of Mommy's

who writes for the *Stoneybrook News* thought the *3M Gazette* was great. She started a kids' page in the grown-up paper. Sometimes I write articles or make up puzzles for the kids' page. I did not have anything in the paper this morning. But it was still fun to read.

I finished the kids' page. Then I flipped through the grown-up news.

"Boring. Boring. Boring," I said as I turned the pages. "Hey, wait!" I cried. "I found something new."

I saw a headline that said: *Your Daily Horoscope*. Below it were short paragraphs in two columns. That was good. It looked easy to read. The other pages in the paper had way too many words.

But I wasn't sure what a horoscope was. So I asked Kristy.

"For every birth date, there is a special sign," said Kristy. "The signs are astrol-al. That means they have something with the stars and planets. All you

have to do is look up the sign for your birthday. Then you can read your horoscope."

I ran my finger down the columns until I found my birthday.

"Listen to my horoscope, everyone. It says, *Today is a day for opening up to others. The results will be rewarding.*"

"I want to hear my horror-soap," said Andrew.

"The word is horoscope," I told him. "If you wait a minute, I will find yours."

Andrew's horoscope said: *"Opportunity awaits you. Watch for the signs."*

I looked up Daddy's sign next. *"It is time to review your finances. Taking risks will produce great profits."*

"Here's yours, Nannie," I said. *"You work hard all week. Make today your special day."*

Kristy's horoscope said she should get out in the fresh air and enjoy nature. David Michael was supposed to look for answers in unexpected places.

I read the horoscopes for everyone at the big house. Then I read Mommy's and Seth's. I would have read the horoscopes for our pets, too. But I was not sure when their birthdays were. Anyway, I had read all the horoscopes on the page.

I went back to eating my Krispy Krunchy cereal. It was still crispy and crunchy. While I ate, I thought about my horoscope. I was supposed to open up to others for rewarding results. I would have to pay close attention today to see if my horoscope came true.

"Ouch!" I cried.

"What is wrong?" asked Daddy.

"Nothing," I replied. I was rubbing my cheek.

Then I thought, this is it! This is my chance to open up to others! So I told Daddy about my tooth.

"Well, be sure to tell your mother tonight. She can make an appointment with the dentist for you," said Daddy.

That night at the little house, I forgot to tell Mommy. Well, I did not really forget. I decided that opening up to Daddy was rewarding enough for one day. Besides, my tooth was not bothering me. So why bother Mommy?

School

On Monday morning at the little house, I read my horoscope. It said, *A friend will help you today.*

Do you know what? My horoscope came true.

On the playground at school, the Three Musketeers were playing hopscotch. All of a sudden Hannie called, "Karen, look out!"

I ducked just in time. A Frisbee whizzed past my head.

On Tuesday, my horoscope said, *You will learn something new today.*

15

I did! I learned how to spell *chrysanthe-mum*.

By Wednesday morning, I did not even have to ask for the horoscope page. Seth put it at my place at the table. (Mommy and Seth get *The New York Times* and *The Hartford Courant* at the little house. The *Times* does not have horoscopes. The *Courant* does.)

This was my horoscope: *Watch out for enemies today.*

Uh-oh. I had a best enemy at school. Pamela Harding. I would have to watch out for her.

I read more horoscopes while I waited for Mommy to drive me to school.

"Are you ready, Karen?" she called.

"In a minute!" I replied.

Reading all those horoscopes had given me an idea. I ran into the playroom and found my crystal ball. I slipped it into my backpack.

That morning, I was the first one in the

classroom. My desk is at the front of the room. I used to sit in the back with Hannie and Nancy. But when I got glasses, Ms. Colman moved me up front. She said I would be able to see better.

The other kids who wear glasses and sit up front are Natalie Springer and Ricky Torres. (Ricky is my pretend husband.)

Addie Sidney sits up front, too. But she has a different kind of desk. It is the tray of her wheelchair. She uses a wheelchair because she has cerebral palsy.

"Hi, Karen!" called Hannie.

I pulled out my crystal ball.

"Hi! Do you want to hear your daily fortune?" I asked.

"Sure," said Hannie.

I had read Hannie's horoscope in the *Courant*. But I checked my crystal ball to make sure it was right.

"The stars and the crystals are in agreement," I said. "A happy surprise awaits you."

"That's neat!" said Hannie. "I can't wait to find out what it is."

Then Nancy came into the room. "What is my fortune?" she asked.

I closed my eyes and passed my hands over the crystal ball.

"Someone close to you will need your help today," I said.

"Hmm. I wonder who will need me," said Nancy.

Ricky arrived with Hank Reubens and Bobby Gianelli. (Hank and Ricky are best friends. Bobby is sometimes a bully.) I checked my crystal ball.

"You will be a winning team today," I said.

Terri and Tammy, the twins, showed up next. Guess who came in behind them. Pamela Harding, Jannie Gilbert, and Leslie Morris. (They are good friends.)

I put my crystal ball away. I did not want Pamela to see it. Today was the day to watch out for my enemy.

Behind Pamela was Ms. Colman, who is the best teacher ever. Later, I would read Ms. Colman's fortune. I would make sure it was a very happy one.

Ouch!

After Ms. Colman took attendance, she made a Surprising Announcement. (I love Surprising Announcements!)

"This afternoon we will have an Autumn Leaves Party," she said.

"Yes!" I cried. Then I added, "Indoor voice, please."

"Thank you, Karen," said Ms. Colman. She was smiling. (I think she was happy I had remembered the indoor voice rule, even though I had forgotten to follow it.)

"This morning we will make leaf decorations. After recess we will bake leaf-shaped cookies," Ms. Colman said.

This was very good news.

"But first we will have our math quiz," added Ms. Colman.

Boo. This was very bad news.

When I got my quiz, I went right to work. I was careful to keep my eyes on my own paper. (I had made the mistake of copying from Ricky before and I had been very sorry.)

The math problems were hard. I had to count on my fingers. My head started to ache. No, wait. It was not my head. It was my tooth again. (I had not remembered to tell Mommy it was bothering me.)

I did not tell Ms. Colman either. I waited for the ache to go away.

My tooth felt better when we started making our autumn leaves. Maybe I was just having too much fun to think about it.

"Would you please pass the brown crayon?" I asked Addie.

"Sure," she replied. "Here is the red one, too. Autumn leaves have lots of red in them." (Addie is very good at arts and crafts.)

By lunchtime, I had made piles of autumn leaves. They were gigundoly beautiful. Ms. Colman strung all the leaves across the room.

When we came back from recess, we baked the cookies. My job was to beat the egg yolks. I am very good at beating eggs. Ms. Colman says it is because I have so much energy.

"Hey, Hannie," I said. "Why are cooks mean?"

"I don't know," said Hannie.

"Because they beat the eggs and whip the cream!" I said.

I just love parties. I love baking cookies. And best of all, I love eating cookies.

When the cookies were all baked and cooled, Ms. Colman gave each of us three on a colored napkin. My first cookie was shaped like a maple leaf. I took a big bite.

I wanted to say, "Yum!" Instead I yelped, "Ouch!"

"Karen, what is wrong?" asked Ms. Colman.

I pointed to my tooth.

"I think you should see the nurse," said Ms. Colman. "Nancy, will you go with Karen, please?"

Nancy walked me to the nurse's office. Then she went back to the party.

"What brings you here, Karen?" asked Ms. Pazden. (She is the school nurse.)

I pointed to my tooth again.

"Is this the first time it has hurt you?" Ms. Pazden asked.

I decided I better tell the truth. I told her about the times it had bothered me.

"I do not want to go to the dentist, though. I do not want to get a filling," I moaned.

"But Karen, your tooth will just keep hurting you if you don't go," she said. She

picked up the phone and called Mommy.

"I think Karen should see her dentist as soon as possible," Ms. Pazden said.

Bullfrogs.

Dr. Rice

Mommy and Andrew were waiting to pick me up after school.

"I am sorry your tooth hurts, Karen," said Mommy. "I am sure Dr. Rice will be able to help."

Dr. Rice is our family dentist. He treats everyone: Mommy, Seth, Andrew, and me.

"Maybe you have a cabity," said Andrew.

"The word is cavity. And maybe I do not have one," I said.

26

I was feeling pretty grumpy. I did not feel like thinking about cabities, or cavities either.

We pulled up in front of Dr. Rice's office. His office is in a white house with blue shutters. Inside, the walls are covered with pictures of people with shiny teeth.

"Hello, Karen," said Dr. Rice. "I hear a tooth has been bothering you lately. Let's see if we can make it feel better."

I followed Dr. Rice down a hallway. I sat in the chair. Dr. Rice stepped on a pedal and the chair sailed up. (That is one part of going to the dentist that I like.)

"Can you point to the tooth that is bothering you, Karen?" asked Dr. Rice.

I pointed.

"Good. Now, if you will open your mouth a bit more, I can take a look at it," said Dr. Rice.

"May I have some water first?" I asked.

"Of course," said Dr. Rice.

There was a sink next to the chair. I pushed a little button and a cup filled up

27

with water. The water did not run over the top. How did it know when to stop? (Filling the water cup is the other part of going to the dentist that I like. But that is all.)

"Ready?" asked Dr. Rice. (He was smiling. He is a very nice man.)

"Ready," I said. I opened my mouth wide.

Dr. Rice tapped my tooth with a shiny metal stick. It did not hurt. My tooth just felt kind of sore.

"I do not see a cavity there. Let me take an X ray. That way we can see inside your tooth," said Dr. Rice.

He put a heavy blanket over me. He said it was to keep me safe from the X rays. Then he put a little card inside my mouth and pointed a big machine at it.

Dr. Rice went out of the room. The machine went *click*. It did not hurt one bit.

When the X ray was ready, Dr. Rice called Mommy and Andrew in to look at it.

"Karen's X ray shows that an adult tooth is waiting underneath her baby tooth," said

Dr. Rice. "The adult tooth is more than ready to come in. It is pressing on the baby tooth. But the baby tooth does not seem ready to come out. The only way to make Karen feel better is to pull out the baby tooth."

That did not sound very nice to me.

"I suggest you see Dr. Celenza," said Dr. Rice. "She is an oral surgeon who specializes in working with children. I will give you her number."

"Thank you, Doctor," said Mommy.

The Fortune-teller

"**W**ell, at least you did not have a cavity. That was good news. Wasn't it, Karen?" asked Mommy. We were in the car on our way home.

"I guess so," I grumbled.

I did not want to have a cavity filled. But I *really* did not want to have a tooth pulled. And I did not want to go to a new dentist. I *know* Dr. Rice. He is nice. I did not know the new doctor at all. Maybe the new doctor would not be so nice.

At home, I ran to my room. I picked up

Hyacynthia. She is the English baby doll I share with Nancy. I knew she would understand about going to doctors. She needed to be repaired by a doll doctor once.

"Open wide, Hyacynthia," I said.

I looked inside her mouth. I did not see any stuck baby teeth.

"You are lucky," I said. "I am not. I need to have my tooth pulled out."

Hyacynthia gave me a hug.

"I knew you would understand," I said.

Ring! Ring! It was the telephone.

In a minute, Mommy called, "It is for you, Karen. It is Nancy."

"Hi, Nancy," I said. "What's up?"

"I am so glad you are home," said Nancy. "I could not wait to talk to you. My fortune came true!"

I had to think for a minute. I could not remember Nancy's fortune.

"You said someone close to me would need my help. Well, Danny pulled on a lamp cord. The lamp was big and heavy. I caught it just in time and saved him!" said Nancy.

Danny is Nancy's baby brother. I was glad she had helped him. I was also amazed that her fortune had come true.

We talked for a little while and I told Nancy about my tooth. Later, I was on my way back to my room when the phone rang again.

"Karen, it is for you. It is Hannie," said Mommy.

"Guess what! My fortune came true," said Hannie.

I remembered Hannie's fortune. "You mean you got a happy surprise?" I asked.

"Yes. My grandma is coming to visit us next weekend. I have not seen her in ages. I am so happy!" said Hannie.

And I am so surprised, I thought. I did not expect my fortunes to come true. I was only playing.

The phone did not ring for five whole minutes. That is because Mommy was calling the new dentist. I heard her make an appointment for me for Monday morning. Boo.

As soon as she hung up, the phone started ringing again.

Ricky told me that he and Bobby and Hank won a game of stickball. (I remembered telling them they would be a winning team.)

And Addie called to say that a new package of stickers had arrived. (I had told her she would get some important mail.)

Maybe I really can predict the future, I thought. Maybe I am a real and true fortune-teller just like Madame Valerie.

Madame Karena Brewena

I had thought fortune-telling was just for fun. But maybe I really *could* predict the future. And why not? I had been reading the horoscopes every day. And I watched Madame Valerie very closely on TV.

I just needed to *look* like a real fortune-teller. And I needed a name.

Let's see. Madame Karen Brewer. No. I needed something more. Karena. Yes. I like it. Karena Brewena. *Madame* Karena Brewena. Perfect!

Now for the clothes. I had a box of dress-up clothes hidden away in my closet. I dragged it out. I found just what I needed. A long, flowery skirt. Six bangle bracelets. Lots of beads. And a scarf for my head.

I put on the clothes. Then I looked in the mirror. Madame Karena Brewena was ready for business.

Andrew was passing by my room.

"Andrew!" I said. "I need someone to practice my fortune-telling on," I said.

"Not me," said Andrew. "I am busy."

"Please? It will be a good fortune," I promised. "Of course I will have to consult my crystal ball to be absolutely sure. But I have a strong feeling that good news awaits you."

"Really? Okay, then. You can tell my fortune," said Andrew.

We went down to the playroom. I put a chair on either side of a small table.

"Please be seated," I said.

I set the crystal ball on the table between us. I thought about Andrew's horoscope in the paper. It had said something about great losses. That was not good news. I looked into my crystal ball. I spoke in my most mysterious voice.

"Tell me! Tell me Andrew Brewer's fortune," I said.

I closed my eyes. Suddenly his fortune came to me.

"You will find something you have been looking for," I said.

"Oh, goody!" exclaimed Andrew. "I lost my spaceman yesterday. Can you ask the crystal ball where it is?"

"The crystal ball has spoken. It will speak no more," I replied.

"Then I am going back upstairs to play," said Andrew.

I decided to find *The Hartford Courant*. If I was going to be a real and true fortune-teller, I needed to study very hard.

I read the horoscopes over again. By

the time I finished, it was bedtime. I stopped by Andrew's room to say good night.

He was already asleep. He was holding something against his chest. I leaned into his room to see better. It was his spaceman. Amazing! My prediction had come true.

Special Powers

On Thursday morning, I woke up early to read the horoscopes. I read each one twice.

"Madame Karena Brewena," I said to myself. "You are ready."

I packed my skirt, scarf, jewelry, and crystal ball into my knapsack.

When I arrived at school, I made my very own Surprising Announcement. (Ms. Colman was not there yet.)

"As many of you have seen, I have special fortune-telling powers. So at lunchtime, I, Madame Karena Brewena, will be waiting on the playground to tell your fortunes. The charge will be twenty-five cents per person."

"Can we get our money back if we don't like our fortune?" asked Bobby Gianelli.

"I am sorry. Fortunes are non-refundable," I said. Then I decided to tell everyone about my tooth.

"If you are interested in having your fortune told, you should take advantage of this amazing offer today. On Monday, I am having a serious dental operation. I may not be able to speak for a long time after."

"You are having an operation?" asked Natalie. Her bottom lip began to quiver. She looked as if she were going to cry. (Natalie cries very easily.)

"Yes. I am having my baby tooth *pulled*," I said.

"Ooh. That sounds scary," said Addie.

"I would not want to have my tooth pulled," said Terri. "I hope you will be okay."

"Will you get money under your pillow from the tooth fairy?" asked Ricky. "I think you should get double for a tooth that is pulled!"

Just then, Ms. Colman came into the room and asked us to take our seats. I told her about my tooth. She wished me good luck.

The morning seemed to go on forever. When recess finally came, I decided to put on my scarf, my skirt, and my jewelry over my regular clothes. (It was cold outside.)

I dragged three plastic milk crates across the playground to the seesaws. They were going to be my table and chairs. I put up a cardboard sign I had made in class that morning:

☆ ☆
☆ **MADAME KARENA BREWENA**
PLAYGROUND FORTUNE-TELLER
25 CENTS A FORTUNE

Hannie was first on line. She handed me her quarter.

I gazed into my crystal ball. "I see numbers. Many numbers," I said. "They add up to a good mark on our next math quiz."

"Thanks, Karen!" said Hannie.

Nancy was behind Hannie. "A letter from an old friend will reach you soon," I said.

It was Ricky's turn. "Today is your day to compliment a friend," I said. (Of course, I hoped the friend would be me.)

Natalie handed me her quarter. She looked a little worried.

I peered into the crystal ball and shook my head sadly. "Madame Brewena is sorry to tell you that you will have the dropsies

MADAME KARENA BREWENA
PLAYGROUND FORTUNE-TELLER
25 CENTS A FORTUNE

today. Watch out when handling glitter at arts and crafts."

"My turn!" said Addie.

"I see paper. I see a pencil. I see letters," I said mysteriously. "You will write a funny poem today."

By the time recess was over, everyone who wanted a fortune, had gotten one.

I was pleased. My first day as playground fortune-teller had gone very well.

A Prediction
for Ms. Colman

On Friday, I was back in business. In the morning, before Ms. Colman arrived, I made an important announcement.

"Your attention, please. Madame Karena Brewena will be available to tell fortunes at recess."

A few kids were not paying attention. So I decided to make another announcement.

"Your attention again, please. It is highly unusual for a fortune-teller to tell her own fortune. But I, Karena Brewena, will do it today! I will read my future in the crystal ball. Do not miss it!"

Pamela, Leslie, and Jannie were off in the corner talking. Luckily, I had one more announcement to make. I knew this one would interest them.

"I would like to add that this morning I had a *feeling*. An important fortune-teller feeling. It is about Ms. Colman. If the feeling continues through the morning, I will make my prediction at recess."

That did it. I had everyone's attention now. Even Pamela, Leslie, and Jannie looked interested.

All morning, when Ms. Colman was not looking, my friends asked me to tell her fortune.

Ricky wrote me a note. It said, "You can tell me. I am your husband."

I wrote back, "Sorry. You have to wait like everyone else."

Finally it was lunchtime. I could hardly eat because everyone was crowding around me. (It is not easy being a world-famous fortune-teller like me.)

When I finished eating, I went into the bathroom and turned myself into Madame Karena. Then I ran straight outside to the seesaws.

A few fortunes were coming in strong. I had to tell them.

"Natalie, I have good news. Your dropsies are over," I said.

"That is a relief," said Natalie. "I was dropping everything yesterday."

"You were right about my fortune, Karen," said Addie. "I wrote a funny poem last night."

"My fortune came true, too," said Hannie. "I got a very good mark on my math quiz."

"That is great, Hannie. According to my crystal ball, you are on a winning streak. You will do well on three more quizzes," I said.

After I told a few more fortunes, I was

ready to tell my own. I rested my hands on my crystal ball. Then I pulled them off as though the crystal ball had turned red-hot.

"I see bad news about my appointment with my new dentist, Dr. Celenza," I said. "It will be a disaster."

"Oh, Karen, that is too bad," said Hannie.

"Maybe it is too hard to tell your own fortune. Maybe it won't come true," said Natalie.

"Right," said Nancy. "Do not worry."

"How about telling us Ms. Colman's fortune now?" said Pamela. "You promised." (Pamela did not seem very worried about my dental disaster.)

"Yes, tell us!" said the other kids. "We want to hear about Ms. Colman."

"I am sorry," I said. "My feeling is not quite strong enough."

"Oh, come on, Karen. You did promise," said Hank.

"I am sorry. You will just have to wait until next week," I replied.

I would know then if my prediction about Dr. Celenza had come true. If it had, then Ms. Colman's prediction was sure to come true, too.

I would have the answer by Monday afternoon.

B-A-B-Y

"Dinner is ready, girls!" called Elizabeth.

It was Friday on a big-house weekend. Mommy had dropped Andrew and me off in the afternoon. Then Nancy and Hannie had come over. That is because Daddy had said I could have a Three Musketeers sleepover.

"Daddy made his special vegetarian chili," I told Nancy and Hannie.

That was one of my favorite meals. There were always so many bowls on the table. Here is what the bowls were filled with:

Chili. Sour cream. Onions. Peppers. Cheddar cheese. Taco shells. (I do not eat the onions or the peppers.)

"Who wants to hear their fortunes?" I asked while we were eating. Everyone did, except Kristy, Sam, and Charlie. Kristy had to leave to baby-sit. Sam and Charlie were going to a movie.

I told everyone else's fortune. (I predicted that Emily Michelle would spill her chili on the floor. And she did.) Then the Three Musketeers ran to my room for our party.

We had brought along the Doll Sisters, Merry, Terry, and Kerry. We bought them together with our very own money. They had not seen each other in ages. They had a lot to catch up on.

After a while, Nancy said to me, "What kind of feeling did you have about Ms. Colman?"

"I am sorry. I am still not ready to talk about it," I replied.

"Oh, come on," said Nancy.

"The feeling is not quite clear," I said.

"But we could ask the Ouija board. I brought it with me."

"That is a good idea," said Hannie. "Let's turn the lights out. The Ouija board always works better when it is dark."

I turned out all the lights, except for one little lamp on my table. I found an old sheet. We hung it over three chairs. Then we climbed into our fortune-telling tent.

I placed my fingertips on the pointer.

"Tell us what you know about Ms. Colman," I said.

Slowly, the pointer slid across the board to the letter B. Then it moved to A. Then back to B. Then to Y. Then it stopped completely.

We said the letters out loud together. B-A-B-Y.

"I knew it!" I cried. "Ms. Colman is going to have a baby!"

"Wow!" said Nancy. "This is exciting!"

"But wait," said Hannie. "If she has a baby, she might leave school."

"She cannot do that. She promised she

would be our teacher even after she got married," I said.

"That was before the Ouija board told us about her baby," replied Hannie.

"Wait till the rest of the kids hear about this," I said.

"Should we call them now?" asked Nancy.

"I do not think so. I think we should wait until Monday to tell them," said Hannie.

"But we will have to wait until after my dentist appointment," I added.

Waiting was not going to be easy. We had found out the secret just five minutes earlier. But it felt like five years.

It was going to be a long weekend.

12

Albert's Toothache

By Sunday night, I was back in my room at the little house. I was thinking about my appointment with Dr. Celenza. I was not just thinking. I was worrying.

"Goosie, I cannot go through with my visit to the dentist. It is going to be a disaster," I said.

Goosie had something to say. I held him up to my ear. He said I should keep my appointment. He said my tooth would feel better if I did.

"But I do not know Dr. Celenza. Maybe

she will make my tooth feel worse," I replied.

I made up my mind about something. I was not going to go to the dentist. I went downstairs to tell Mommy and Seth.

"Karen, honey, you have to go. It is the only way your tooth will feel better," said Mommy. "Dr. Celenza works with children all the time. She is a very good dentist."

"I know going to the dentist can be scary," said Seth. "Before I had a cap put on my tooth, I was nervous all day."

"I have an idea," said Mommy. "Tomorrow I will bake you an I-went-to-the-dentist cake. It will have icing and candles and everything."

"Thank you. But I am not going," I said.

"It is time for bed now, Karen. I got a new book for you from the library. I think you will like it," said Mommy.

The book was called *Albert's Toothache*. It was by Barbara Williams. It was about a turtle who says he has a toothache. But tur-

56

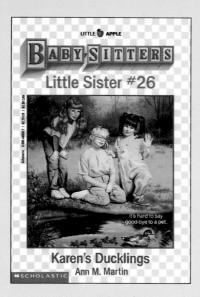

#26

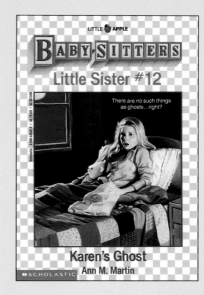

#12

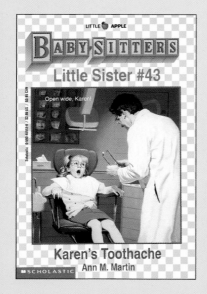

#43

#34

Gooooood Sandwich!

To make this hauntingly good treat you will need one slice of white or wheat bread, raisins, cream cheese, and a knife.

Use the knife to cut a ghost shape from the bread. Spread cream cheese on top of your bread–ghost. Use the raisins to make the ghost's eyes, nose, and mouth.

Boo! This ghost is good to chew!

Where Egg–zactly Are They?

There are six eggs hidden in this spring scene. Can you find them all?

Tell the Tooth Jokes!

The dentist may tell you to cut down on eating sweets, but no one will tell you to stop laughing at these funny dessert jokes.

What is a frog's favorite candy?
Lollihops.

Waiter, this doughnut is crushed!
Well, you said, "Bring me a doughnut – and step on it!"

Why did the apple kiss the banana?
Because it had a-peel!

tles do not have teeth. It turns out he really has a sore toe because a gopher bit him.

"That was a good story, Mommy," I said. "But I have a real toothache in my real mouth and I *really* do not want to go to the dentist."

"Get some rest now," said Mommy. "I will see you in the morning."

As soon as Mommy left my room, I turned the light back on. If I was going to the dentist the next day, I had to do something important right away.

I found some paper and a pen. At the top of a page I wrote in big letters:

KAREN BREWER'S LAST WILL AND TESTAMENT

(I did not know what a testament was. But I saw that word in a book once. It sounded important.)

On the first line, I started to make a list of all my earthly possessions. They were Goosie, Moosie, Tickly, Hyacynthia, Terry, pink sneakers, pink unicorn shirt, strawberry eraser, lucky hopscotch stone, bicycle, crystal ball . . .

The list was getting very long. I crossed everything out and wrote:

HEAR YE! HEAR YE! I, KAREN BREWER, LEAVE ALL MY STUFF TO KRISTY THOMAS, MY BIG STEPSISTER. (PLEASE LET ANDREW AND HANNIE AND NANCY PICK WHAT THEY WANT FIRST.)

Nancy would take Hyacynthia. We share her anyway. But who would get Goosie and Moosie? And I wanted the pieces of Tickly to go to people who would appreciate him. I needed to write that down.

This was getting complicated. I would have to leave it up to Kristy.

Now for the service. I wanted it to be a nice one. I wanted everyone to come. My two families. My neighbors. Ms. Colman. All the kids in my class.

I was sure Pamela Harding would cry the hardest. That is because she would be sorry she has been so mean to me.

Poor Ricky. I hoped he would marry again someday. (But not too soon.)

Of course, everyone would say gigundoly nice things about me. They would remember what a good fortune-teller I was. Too bad she had a terrible toothache, they would say.

The world without Karen Brewer would be a sorry place. I wiped a couple of tears off my cheek. If my dentist visit turned out to be a disaster, there would not be a dry eye left in Stoneybrook.

Hiding

It was very early Monday morning. I had not slept well. Now I had to make up my mind. And I did. I was not going to go to the dentist.

"I know you do not approve, Goosie. And I am sorry. But I just cannot do it," I said.

I knew I could not tell Mommy and Seth. They would make me go. So I did not say anything at breakfast.

"Are they taking your tooth away today?" asked Andrew.

60

"I do not want to talk about it," I replied. (At least I was not lying to Andrew.)

"Come, Andrew. Time for you to get ready for school," said Mommy.

While Mommy was helping Andrew, I ran upstairs to my room. I bundled myself up in my warmest clothes. I put on two pairs of socks, a turtleneck shirt, a sweater, a sweat shirt, a jacket, gloves, and a hat. I did not want to have to come back home just because I was cold.

I looked out the window. There it was. My hiding place. It was a tree with big, sturdy branches.

I slipped downstairs and out the back door. Then I climbed up the tree in the backyard. (It was hard to do with all those clothes on.)

Soon I heard Seth's car door slam. I heard him start the motor. I watched Seth drive down the street to work. I waved to him. " 'Bye, Seth."

Honk! Honk! It was Andrew's carpool. I watched him climb into the car. I waved again, even though I knew he could not see me. " 'Bye, Andrew."

The next thing I heard was Mommy calling, "Karen, I am going outside to warm up the car now."

I sat very still. I only moved to look at my watch. It was nine o'clock.

Soon, Mommy went back into the house. I knew she was going upstairs to get me. I felt bad that I was not there. But I would feel worse if I had to go to the dentist.

"Karen! Karen, where are you?" called Mommy.

I wished I had brought earmuffs. I did not want to hear Mommy calling me. First she sounded scared. Then she sounded angry. Then she sounded scared again. Finally, she stopped calling.

I looked at my watch. Nine-fifteen. My appointment was supposed to be at nine-thirty.

Nine-thirty came and went. By 9:45, I knew I had missed my appointment with Dr. Celenza.

Suddenly I saw Seth's car pull back into the driveway. Mommy must have called him from work and asked him to come home. Uh-oh. That meant I was in Very Big Trouble.

I climbed down from my hiding place. I walked into the kitchen. Seth was on the phone.

"Hello? Is this the police?" he was saying. "I am calling to report a missing child."

Very Big Trouble

"Young lady, where have you been?" said Mommy. "We were worried sick."

"Thank you anyway, officer. We found her," said Seth. Then he hung up the phone.

"I was in the backyard. I was up in the tree, hiding," I admitted. I stared at the floor.

"We did not know *what* had happned to you," said Mommy. "I called Daddy. I called Nancy's family and Hannie's. I even called school."

"I am sorry," I said.

"Just because you were hiding," said Mommy, "Seth had to leave work, a lot of people are worried, and you missed your dental appointment. I am going to have to punish you, Karen. But first I am going to call Dr. Celenza."

I listened while Mommy called the dentist. She apologized for missing the appointment. Then she made another appointment for Thursday after school.

That sounded like a bad enough punishment to me. I would have to go to the dentist after all. I could not hide again because Mommy was going to pick me up at school.

"You will have to apologize to Dr. Celenza yourself, Karen," said Mommy. "I want you to write a note to her. Tell her why you missed your appointment."

"I will write a very nice letter. I promise," I said. I thought I was getting off easy.

"I am not finished," Mommy went on. "You may not play with your friends after

66

school this week. And now, it is time to go to school."

Boo. Boo. Boo. I did not say one word the whole way there.

When I arrived at school, everyone stared at me.

"We are glad to see you," said Ms. Colman. "We did not expect you until this afternoon. I hope everything went all right at the dentist."

I did not want the class to know about my morning. So I just nodded and sat down at my desk. I was very, very hot. (I was still wearing two pairs of socks, my turtleneck, and my sweater.)

At lunchtime, I told Nancy and Hannie what I had done.

"So we can't play all week," I explained.

"That is too bad," said Nancy.

"Do you still want to tell the kids Ms. Colman's news after lunch?" asked Hannie.

It took me a minute to remember Ms. Colman's news. Oh, right. We spelled out

B-A-B-Y on the Ouija board. That seemed like a hundred years ago.

"I think my powers are fading. I am not so sure about my prediction for Ms. Colman. Maybe we should not say anything yet," I said.

"Okay. We will wait until your powers come back," said Hannie.

"We have plenty of time," added Nancy. "It will be our secret for now."

The Return
of the Powers

When I woke up on Tuesday, I was not alone. I could feel the presence of Madame Karena Brewena. My powers had returned.

Mommy and Seth were not so mad at me anymore. I did not complain once about my punishment. And I had apologized so many times at dinner the night before, they just had to forgive me.

I still did not want to go to the dentist, though. But I knew I was going. On Thursday. And that was that.

At breakfast, I wore my beads and bangles and read the horoscopes.

Then I packed my crystal ball in my knapsack and Mommy drove me to school.

"Madame Karena Brewena is back," I announced when I walked into my classroom. "My special powers have returned. They are stronger than ever! If you want to hear important news, meet me by the seesaws at recess."

By the time the kids were leaving the lunch room that afternoon, I was set up on the playground and ready for business.

"Once again, I will tell my own fortune first," I announced. I touched my forehead to the crystal ball. I moaned pitifully.

"Disaster. I see disaster at the dentist on Thursday," I said. (Most of the kids knew that I had not yet had my tooth pulled.)

"You must try to be brave," said Natalie.

"Yes, I will," I replied.

"Is the crystal ball giving you any other message?" asked Hannie.

I closed my eyes and threw back my head.

"Yes! Yes!" I replied. "The crystal ball says I am right about Ms. Colman. It says this is the time to tell everyone her news."

I opened my eyes and looked at my classmates. When I thought they could not wait a second longer, I made the most Surprising Announcement of all.

"Ms. Colman is going to have a baby," I said.

"Wow! Are you sure?" asked Addie.

"The crystal ball does not lie," I replied.

"When will the baby be born?" asked Jannie.

"Oh, the usual. In eight or nine months. The crystal ball may not have given me the news right away," I said.

"Do you know whether it will be a boy or a girl?" asked Leslie.

"It will definitely be one or the other."

"Will Ms. Colman still be our teacher?" asked Bobby.

"Oh, yes. She will have to be our teacher. She promised."

"This is awesome!" said Tammy.

"Are you sure about this, Karen?" asked Pamela. "Maybe you got your signals scrambled."

"My signals are coming through loud and clear," I told her.

"I wonder how Ms. Colman is feeling," said Ricky. "She has to be careful now. She has to rest and take it easy. We have to be extra nice to her."

"You are right, Ricky," I said. "Ms. Colman has to take good care of herself from now on. It will be our job to help her."

"Be Careful!"

When we returned to our classroom on Tuesday, we found Ms. Colman reaching way back into the supply closet.

"Ms. Colman, be careful!" I cried. "I will get whatever you need."

"Why, thank you, Karen," said Ms. Colman. "We are going to make a chart about the life cycle of a leaf. I need some colored markers."

When everyone was seated, Ms. Colman picked up the giant pad of paper we use for class charts.

"Oh, no, no, no!" we cried. "We will carry that for you. Please, Ms. Colman. You really have to be careful."

We watched over our teacher for the rest of the afternoon.

On Wednesday, Ricky pulled Ms. Colman's chair out for her when she wanted to sit at her desk.

"You should be sitting as much as possible now," he said.

I thought that was very good advice. But Ms. Colman was not a good listener. The next thing we knew, she was trying to stand on a chair by the bulletin board.

I thought Ricky would have a heart attack.

"Wait! Stop!" he cried. "You have to be careful!"

"Yes, you told me that yesterday," said Ms. Colman. "But I need to hang up this chart."

"We will help you," I said.

"I do not know why you are all so worried about me," said Ms. Colman.

On Thursday morning, we pulled out Ms. Colman's chair. We would not let her carry anything heavier than a pencil. We made her sit down most of the day. And we told her to "Be careful!" about a million times.

At recess, Pamela Harding had a very good idea. (Even a best enemy can have a good idea sometimes.) She said we should plan a baby shower for Ms. Colman.

"This will be her first baby," said Pamela. "She will need *every*thing."

"We should find out what she wants," I said.

"But we cannot let her know why we are asking," added Nancy.

That afternoon, Ms. Colman was writing our new spelling words on the blackboard. (We asked her to sit down while she wrote them, but she said she could not.)

One of our spelling words was purple. Perfect!

"Ms. Colman, if you were a boy, would you rather wear blue, green, or purple?" I asked.

"That is an excellent sentence for the word purple," said Ms. Colman.

"Thank you. But I need to know the answer," I said. "Which color would you like to wear if you were a boy?"

"Blue, I suppose," Ms. Colman replied patiently.

"Speaking of colors," said Pamela, "which toy would you rather have — a green rattle, or a brown bear?"

"I think bears are nice toys. Now may we please get back to our spelling words?" said Ms. Colman.

"How about bibs?" said Hannie. "Do you like the squeaky kind?"

Ms. Colman rolled her eyes. "You kids are acting very strange these days," she said. "Very nice. But very strange."

The Amazing Dr. Celenza

It was Thursday afternoon. The time had come. There was no getting out of it.

Mommy and Andrew were waiting outside school for me. They were waiting to take me downtown to Dr. Celenza.

We reached her office and walked inside. The waiting room was nothing great. I saw a few more toys than usual. But that was all.

Soon someone poked his head through the doorway and called, "Karen Brewer?"

Then he came into the waiting room to get me.

"I am Jonathan, Dr. Celenza's assistant," he said. He was wearing an astronaut's suit that was covered with gold and silver stars. But he was not wearing a helmet, and I could see he was smiling.

"Right this way," he said.

Jonathan led me to Dr. Celenza's office. I felt as if I were in outer space. The walls were covered with colored stars. They were red, green, yellow, and blue. A moon hung from the ceiling. All around were pictures of smiling kids. The best part was the chair. It looked like a rocketship. It even had a make-believe control panel. While I was pushing the buttons on the panel, Dr. Celenza came in.

"Hello, Karen," she said. "I am glad to meet you."

I liked her right away. First of all, she did not say one word about missing my Monday appointment. And I liked the way

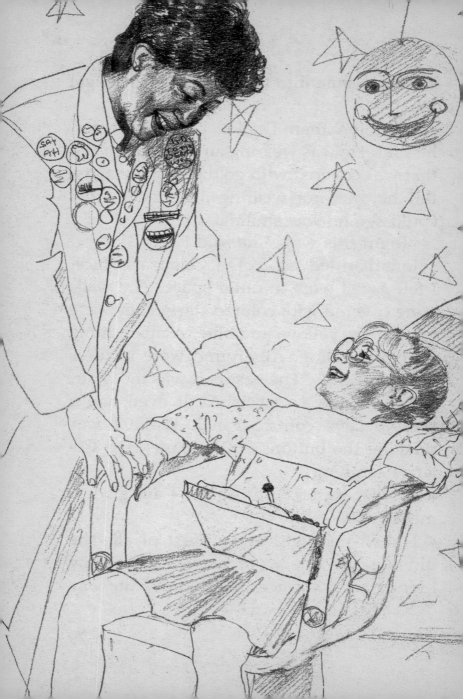

she was dressed. She was wearing a white doctor's coat, but it was covered with funny buttons. My favorite one said, "Go to the dentist? Who me?"

"Hi," I replied. "Does this chair go up and down?"

"Hang on to your hat," said Dr. Celenza. "I am going to give you a ride."

She did not give me one ride. She gave me three rides up and down.

"Now it is time for some 'sleepy tooth,' " said Dr. Celenza. "That is a quick shot of novocaine. After that, you will not feel a thing."

That sounded good to me. Before I could count all the stars on the walls, my tooth was out and my visit was over. I had felt a little bit of pressure, but having my tooth pulled had not hurt one bit.

Before I left, Dr. Celenza gave me a present. It was my tooth on a chain. And that was not all. She let me choose a prize for being such a good patient.

Jonathan held out a space helmet. In it was the all-time best prize selection ever. (I picked a star stamp and a pad of red ink.)

When I went back to the waiting room, I was smiling from ear to ear.

I showed Mommy and Andrew my tooth. It was hanging around my neck.

"I love Dr. Celenza!" I said. "She is the best dentist ever."

I was glad my baby tooth was out. I did not need it anymore. I thought of one other thing I did not need. My will.

I decided I would tear it into tiny little pieces.

18

Mush for Dinner

By the time I returned home, my "sleepy tooth" was waking up. My mouth felt a little sore. But that was all.

I ate some Jell-O. Then Mommy said, "Why don't you lie on the couch until supper is ready?"

That sounded like a very good idea to me. After all, I had just had a serious operation.

I brought a funny book called *Beezus and Ramona* by Beverly Cleary with me. I brought paper and markers in case I wanted to draw. And I invited Hyacynthia to keep me company.

Andrew wanted to keep me company, too. He wanted to know what having a tooth pulled out felt like.

"Well, the first thing is, you have to be very brave. They strap you into a big rocketship chair," I explained.

Andrew nodded. He looked thoughtful.

"Did the operation hurt much?" asked Andrew.

"No. Dr.Celenza put my tooth to sleep. It really did not hurt at all," I replied. (I did not want to scare Andrew.) "But you still have to be very brave because it *could* hurt," I added. (I did not want him to think it was so easy either.)

"Then what?" asked Andrew.

"Well, then the dentist pulls out your tooth and hangs it on a chain," I said. "And now, I think I need to rest. Having a tooth pulled out can make you very tired."

I really was pretty tired. I closed my eyes for a minute. Then I opened them again and called, "Mommy!"

Mommy came into the room.

"Are you all right?" she asked.

"How will I be able to eat supper? There is a big hole where my tooth used to be," I said. "Plus, my mouth hurts."

"No problem," said Mommy. "We have already taken care of it. Seth is putting your supper through the blender right now."

I could hear the blender whirring in the kitchen.

"Would you like to eat your supper here as a special treat? Or would you rather join us at the table?" asked Mommy.

"I will come to the table," I said. (I was tired of lying on the couch.)

A plate was set at every place, except mine. At mine was a bowl. And I did not have a knife and fork. I had a spoon. I was having mush for dinner.

Do you know what? It tasted very good.

By the time I went upstairs to bed that night, I had completely recovered from my operation.

I found my will and tore it into little pieces. I was glad I did not need it.

Goosie asked to see the hole where my tooth had been. I opened wide and showed him. I could tell he was impressed.

"Would you like to wear my tooth tonight?" I asked.

He said he would love to, so I hung it around his neck.

"I will have to take it back tomorrow," I said. "In school I am going to show everyone my tooth, the big hole in my mouth, and the prize I got for being such a wonderful patient. I know my friends will want to see everything."

The Tooth Necklace

When I walked into my classroom on Friday, I opened my jacket and cried, "Taa-daa!"

I held up my beautiful tooth necklace. Everyone crowded around to see it.

"That is so cool," said Hannie. "Were you scared?"

"I was a little scared at first," I said. "But as soon as I sat down in the rocketship — "

"Rocketship? What rocketship?" asked Natalie.

"Dr. Celenza's chair is a rocketship," I explained. "Look at the prize I got for being such a good patient."

I showed everyone my star stamp and ink pad.

"Can we see the hole where your tooth was?" asked Nancy.

"Everybody who wants to see it, line up in front of me," I said.

All the kids lined up. I felt gigundoly important. I was being treated like a real and true heroine.

That reminded me of something. Madame Karena Brewena, the real and true fortune-teller, had made a prediction about her visit to Dr. Celenza. The prediction was that the visit was going to be a disaster. Well, it had not been a disaster at all. Boy, had that prediction been wrong.

I wanted to tell Hannie and Nancy about this. I waited until everyone had seen my toothhole. Then I pulled my best friends

aside and whispered my secret to them.

Hannie and Nancy were not the only ones who heard me. A few other kids who were standing around us heard, too.

"That was not the only prediction that was wrong," said Pamela. "You told me to expect a surprise visitor yesterday. No one ever came." Pamela did not look very happy.

"And you said I would win again at stick-ball," said Ricky. "My team got creamed."

Uh-oh, I thought.

"It seems my fortune-telling has been a little off lately," I said. "Maybe Ms. Colman is not having a baby after all."

"Did you bring your crystal ball to school today?" asked Addie. "Maybe you should try again."

"Yes. I have everything I need in my backpack," I replied.

"Then you better consult your crystal ball on the playground after lunch," said Addie.

I knew Addie was right. I promised to be by the seesaws at recess.

Fuzzy

I was on the playground, sitting on my milk crate. My skirt and scarf were blowing in the wind. My beads and bangles clinked together as I passed my hands over the crystal ball.

My classmates had gathered around me. They were waiting for Madame Karena Brewena's latest prediction.

I closed my eyes and concentrated. Then I opened my eyes and peered into the crystal ball. Hmm. I was having trouble seeing anything. I closed my eyes again.

93

I opened them. Closed them. Opened them.

I took my glasses off and wiped them a few times.

"What about Ms. Colman?" asked Natalie.

I shrugged my shoulders. "I cannot tell. Everything is fuzzy," I said.

"We have to know if Ms. Colman is really going to have a baby," said Addie. "If your crystal ball cannot tell us, I will ask her after recess."

Leave it to Addie. If there is a tough question to be asked, Addie will ask it. One time, everyone wanted to know the name of the man Ms. Colman was marrying. We had been calling him the Mystery Man because we were afraid to ask. But not Addie. She asked Ms. Colman. And that is how we found out his name was Mr. Henry Simmons.

As soon we were back in our classroom, Addie raised her hand.

"Ms. Colman, I was thinking," said Addie. "I mean, we were all thinking . . ."

"Yes. Go ahead," said Ms. Colman.

"We were thinking that maybe you are pregnant. Are you pregnant?" asked Addie.

(All right, Addie Sidney!)

Ms. Colman smiled. "No," she said. "I am not pregnant. Mr. Simmons and I hope to have a baby one day. But it will not be for quite a while. We are not ready to start a family yet."

Oops. I had made another wrong prediction. And now my crystal ball was fuzzy.

Well, I did not mind that Ms. Colman was not pregnant. That meant that she would stay and be our teacher.

I did not mind that my appointment with Dr. Celenza had not been a disaster either. Not one bit.

Maybe it was time to give up fortune-telling. Being Madame Karena Brewena was fun. Thinking about the future was fun.

But thinking about the present is fun, too. For the present I was happy to be just plain Karen Brewer. I was happy to look at my very own tooth necklace. Now I would not have a toothache anymore. There would be room for my new grown-up tooth to come in.

What a relief. I smiled a grown-up smile.

About the Author

ANN M. MARTIN lives in New York City and loves animals, especially cats. She has two cats of her own, Mouse and Rosie.

Other books by Ann M. Martin that you might enjoy are *Stage Fright*; *Me and Katie (the Pest)*; and the books in *The Baby-sitters Club* series.

Ann likes ice cream and *I Love Lucy*. And she has her own little sister, whose name is Jane.

Little Sister

Don't miss #44

KAREN'S BIG WEEKEND

"Karen, Andrew," she said. "Seth and I have a surprise for you."

Andrew and I stopped looking at the snow. "You do?" I said.

"Yes," replied Mommy. She sat down. "In one week we will have a special Christmas treat. We are going to go to New York City for the weekend. We will look at the big Christmas tree and see the other decorations. And we will go to the theatre to see a play."

Mommy and Seth told us some more about our trip. They talked about museums and Central Park and glittery Christmas decorations and a Santa Claus on every street corner.

I decided this was going to be the best Christmas ever.

BABY-SITTERS
Little Sister™
by Ann M. Martin, author of *The Baby-sitters Club*®

More Titles... ➡